Farmer Ben's Field

Stories by Norah Clegg and Don Hughes

Pictures by Steve Smallman

Stories in this book

Oliver & Boyd

In Farmer Ben's Field

In the very tall grass
in the corner of
Farmer Ben's field
there was a very special place.

It belonged to
all the animals
who once lived
in the little green wood.
The wood had been chopped down
to make way
for the new motorway.

Willy the weasel
lived in the very tall grass.

Mitzy the mouse
lived in the very tall grass.

Bob the bobtail rabbit
lived in the very tall grass.

Gerty the grass snake
lived in the very tall grass.

The bees, the butterflies
and the birds
lived in the hedgerow
by this special place
in the very tall grass
in the corner of
Farmer Ben's field.

They were all good friends.

They played games.

They had picnics.

They helped each other.

They were very happy.

But one day they
heard a dreadful noise.
Was it another motorway?
No, it was a tractor.
Farmer Ben
was cutting down
the very tall grass.

"Whatever can we do?"
cried the animals.
"Don't worry, don't worry,"
sang the birds.
"We will help."

11

Quickly they gathered
sticks and twigs
and bits of wool.
They made lots of nests.
Some birds sat on the nests.
The other birds flew around
Farmer Ben.
They flew in front of
the tractor.

Farmer Ben
scratched his head.
"Whatever is the matter?
The birds are busy,"
said Farmer Ben.
He looked in the
very tall grass.

He saw the nests.

"My, my," he said.

"It's a good job I stopped!
I might have
spoilt the nests."

He turned his tractor round
and went away.
The special place
in the very tall grass
was safe again.

"Thank you, thank you, birds,"
called out all the animals.
"Do come to our party tonight.
It starts at ten o'clock
when the moon shines bright."
"We will, we will," sang the birds.
And they did!

Dance around the Moon

In the very tall grass
in the corner of
Farmer Ben's field,
all the animals
who lived in this special place
were having a meeting.

It was party time.

At ten o'clock that night,

the moon was shining bright.

"Where will the party be?"
said Willie the weasel.
"What will we do
at our party?"
said Gerty the grass snake.

"We'll dance, dance, dance
around the moon,"
said Bob the bobtail rabbit.
"Dance, dance, dance
around the moon?"
asked the butterflies and birds.
"Impossible!
Even **we** can't fly to the moon."

"Impossible," said
Willie the weasel.
"We haven't got a rocket."

"Impossible," said
all the animals
who lived in
the very tall grass
in the corner of
Farmer Ben's field.

"Come with me.
Come with me,"
said Bob the bobtail rabbit.
"You'll see, you'll see.
We **will** dance
around the moon."

Willie the weasel,
Mitzy the mouse,
Gerty the grass snake and
all the birds and butterflies,
followed Bob the bobtail rabbit.

They climbed over
the stile
in Farmer Ben's field.

They crossed the bridge
over the stream.

They came to a busy road.
"Stop, stop,"
said Bob the bobtail rabbit.
"Remember the Green Cross Code."

This is the Green Cross Code.

First find a safe place to cross, then stop.

Stand on the pavement near the kerb.

Look all round for traffic and listen.

If traffic is coming, let it pass. Look all round again.

When there is no traffic near, walk straight across the road.

Keep looking and listening for traffic while you cross.

They followed Bob the bobtail rabbit
all the way
up the grassy slope
and they all rolled down
the other side.

At the bottom
of the slope
there was the moon
in the middle of
the big blue pond.
"Impossible to dance
around the moon?
Just come with me.
I'll show you!"

Then Bob the bobtail rabbit,
Willie the weasel,
Mitzy the mouse,
Gerty the grass snake and
all the birds and butterflies,
did dance around the moon.